A WORLD WAR II STORY

Across the Blue Pacific

by **LOUISE BORDEN**   Illustrated by **ROBERT ANDREW PARKER**

HOUGHTON MIFFLIN COMPANY • BOSTON 2006

The author would like to thank the United States Naval Academy Alumni Office, the Operational Archives Branch of the Naval Historical Center / Washington Navy Yard, St. Teresa of Avila School, Beechwood School, Bill and Louise Walker, Phyllis Langner, Cynthia Storrs, Walnut Hills High School, Terri Pytlik, Phyllis Hoffman, Betty Carey, Mac Benedict, Martha Tuttle, the editorial and design team at Houghton Mifflin, and especially Bob Parker and Eleni Beja.

www.houghtonmifflinbooks.com

The text of this book is set in Palatino and Agenda.

The illustrations are watercolor.

Library of Congress Cataloging-in-Publication Data

Borden, Louise.
Across the blue Pacific : a World War II story / by Louise Borden ; illustrated by Robert Andrew Parker.
p. cm.
Summary: A woman reminisces about her neighbor's son, who was the object of a letter writing campaign by some fourth-graders when he went away to war in 1943.
ISBN 0-618-33922-1
1. World War, 1939–1945—Juvenile fiction. [1. World War, 1939–1945—Fiction. 2. Letter writing—Fiction. 3. Grief—Fiction. 4. Soldiers—Fiction.] I. Parker, Robert Andrew, ill. II. Title.
PZ7.B64827Ac 2006
[Fic]—dc22

Manufactured in China

SCP 10 9 8 7 6 5 4 3 2 1

ISBN-13: 978-0618-33922-8

For Cate, Ayars, and Ted
— L.B.

For my brother Bill, U.S.N., WWII
— R.A.P.

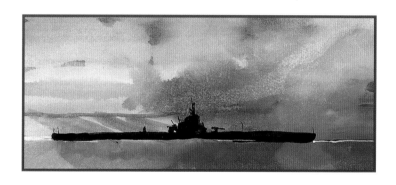

*I*n 1944,
America was still at war
in Europe and in the Pacific.
People said that our country and the Allies
were finally winning
against Germany and Japan.
So did the newspapers and newsreels.
When I was a student at Beechwood School,
everyone in my class
knew a soldier or sailor in uniform.
The U.S. serviceman that I knew
was Lieutenant Ted Walker,
my next-door neighbor on Orchard Road…

Ted Walker was a navy man.
While he was away at college in Maryland,
my brother, Sam, and I were still learning
how to tie our own shoes.
That's when Ted's mother, who was a widow,
got a border collie to keep her company.
When Ted came home on a school vacation,
he named the new puppy Buttons
because he said her eyes were as shiny
as the buttons on his Naval Academy coat.

Ted graduated from Annapolis,
and months later
America entered a big war — World War II.
On that December day in 1941,
Ted was already on duty in the South Atlantic,
standing watch on the deck of the USS *Memphis.*

Those years were full of hard times
for many, many people all over the world.
But my brother, Sam, and I were just kids,
and Orchard Road seemed the safest place on earth,
and the war . . . well, the war was something far away.

In the winter of 1943,
after he finished training in submarines,
Ted Walker came home on leave.
The word spread in a jiffy up and down our street.
Kids in our neighborhood *always* wanted to be around Ted,
and we asked him a hundred questions.

We learned that navy cruisers were named for cities,
and that submarines were named for fish.
If an American sub sank an enemy vessel,
her sailors tied special flags to the conning tower
when they sailed back to port—
flags that told which kind of boat their sub had sunk.

"I'll show you kids how to make a snowsailor,"
Ted told us one Sunday.
Then he topped our snowman with his officer's hat.
"Now he's a lieutenant, just like you," Sam said.
"You bet, Crenshaw," Ted said with a wink
and gave my brother a thumbs-up.
Ted told us we'd each grown "half a fathom."
Then he gave me a lesson or two
on how to polish my Sunday-best shoes.
"Put a little more spit on those, Crenshaw!"
Yes indeed, Sam and I were crazy about Ted Walker.

*I*n March,
Ted's leave ended.
His new navy orders
sent him to another ocean —
this time, the Pacific.

On a wet, windy day,
Sam and I stood in our front yard and waved
until the Walkers' car was just a dark speck
at the end of our street.
We all knew that Ted would be going far away,
that he wouldn't be able to come home anytime soon.
Our dad told us that Ted would cross thousands of miles of ocean.
Thousands of miles on a submarine.
Sam and I told Dad not to worry.
We knew a lot about our country's ships.
They were stronger and faster than ever.
And new subs were as long as a football field.

Sam and I began writing letters to Ted,
and Ted's mother helped us address them.
I always drew a little sketch of Buttons
in the corner on each envelope
and signed my name, *From Molly.*

On summer days after Ted went overseas,
we listened to the radio on Mrs. Walker's porch.
Ted's mother made the best lemonade on the street.
"It's . . . it's a *HOME RUN!*
And the Reds beat the Pirates . . . eight to seven!"
That front porch echoed with our loud cheers.

In wartime,
small victories became big things to celebrate.

And of course,
there was Beechwood School.
Other things were different,
but school was school.
A third grade year flew by for me,
and a first grade year for Sam.
Fathom.
One day I looked up Ted's word in the dictionary.
I was growing taller, but not half a fathom.

Then Mrs. Walker showed us a letter from Hawaii,
written in Ted's scrawly handwriting.
Now Ted was second in command aboard the USS *Albacore.*
I liked the name *Albacore.*
I hoped it would bring Ted good luck.

In September of 1944,
I began fourth grade in Mrs. Linsay's class.
Everyone at Beechwood School knew Mrs. Linsay.
She was strict in a soft kind of way,
and her pet subjects were letter writing
and maps.

The week before,
Mrs. Linsay and some student volunteers
had painted a map of the world
on one of the hallways.
They finished their careful work
just in time for the first day of school.

It was the biggest map any of us at Beechwood had ever seen.
It stretched from the floor to the ceiling
and all the way down the hall.
Every country in the world was on that map.
And a lot of the map was painted blue for the oceans.
The Pacific was the biggest.
It was huge . . .

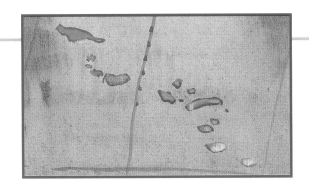

Every time I walked past Mrs. Linsay's map,
I thought about Ted and his submarine,
cruising those Pacific waters.

I pictured the *Albacore,*
long and low on the horizon,
coming into Pearl Harbor
for fuel or supplies or a rest.
I knew her American flag would be flying.
And maybe other flags, too.

Sometimes I stopped and drew a line with my finger
across that smooth wall of blue
from the islands of Hawaii to other U.S. islands:
Midway
and Wake
and Guam.

Dozens of Pacific islands were held by the Japanese.
Some of their names matched the names of terrible battles.
There were so many islands.

Submarines like Ted's *Albacore*
were helping to capture those islands back,
rescuing pilots shot down over the sea
or figuring out where the enemy fleets were.

When Mrs. Linsay asked us to write letters
to servicemen overseas,
I knew right away who to write to.
My friends Amy and F.G. wrote to Ted Walker, too.

We imagined the *Albacore* on patrol,
alone in that ocean.
Just one submarine and one crew
living together, close as a family,
in a steamy narrow space
full of engines and pipes and gauges and dials . . .
with that periscope coming up to take an important look,
turning, turning again,
always watching for other ships . . .
maybe a whole convoy . . . or just one boat.

You had to be brave
to go out on patrol for weeks at a time.
No letters.
No word from home.
You had to be even braver
to dive down into cold, dark water,
down…down…hundreds of feet down.
Diving…diving…
bow pointed down,
feet braced against the steep dive.

You had to be smart, too,
to outfox the enemy ships,
to be as quiet as you could be,
to catch those enemy ships by surprise,
keeping your torpedoes ready,
then firing them,
like fast underwater arrows,
straight to the mark.

My friends and I wrote to Ted every week,
and I always drew my sketches of Buttons.
I hoped our fourth grade letters would be there,
stacked up,
the next time the *Albacore* returned to port.

The school days moved on by,
with reading and math, recess and art.
A thousand leaves rattled into the corners
of the playground.
And on rainy November days,
I was glad to be indoors.
Somehow Mrs. Linsay's classroom
made our world feel cozy and safe.

And then it was December,
just two days before Christmas.
It snowed all morning in swirls of flakes
and gusts of wind,
and the houses were bright with lights
up and down Orchard Road.
But when Sam and I looked out across the side yard,
things didn't seem quite right
at Mrs. Walker's house.
There were too many cars in her driveway
for such a snowy day.

We pulled on our coats
without even buttoning them
and hurried next door.
It was so quiet and still outside,
such a hushed world of snow.
And yet it seemed to me as if my heart
were beating as loud as a drum.

We stood on the porch,
stamped the snow from our wet shoes,
and rang the doorbell.
Ring ring ring…
Ring ring…
The sound echoed in the morning silence.
We saw Buttons through the front window,
and then Ted's two older brothers and their wives.
Ted's favorite uncle,
bald Uncle Will,
opened the door for us.
His face was full of tears.
A telegram had come from the United States Navy…
the kind of message that had not yet come
to a house on our street:

...MISSING IN ACTION AS OF 12 DECEMBER 1944,
HAVING BEEN SERVING ABOARD THE USS ALBACORE
WHEN THAT SUBMARINE FAILED TO RETURN FROM A
WAR PATROL IN THE NORTHWESTERN PACIFIC OCEAN...

Missing.
It seemed like such a little word
for such a big thing.

Maybe the crew had gotten off the *Albacore* safely
and were on an island.
Maybe they had been captured but were still alive.
Maybe…
Maybe…

I wanted to find that terrible telegram
and tear it up into a million yellow pieces.
I wanted to go out
and shout against the cold sky:
Where are you, Ted?
Where are you?
But I didn't want Ted's mother,
Mrs. Walker,
to hear.

The next few days dragged by,
one at a time,
and they weren't filled with any holiday joy.
Just dark gray mornings
when everybody woke up,
hoping.

Slowly,
slowly,
our lives became steadier.
The winter days blurred into a muddy spring,
and it was July again on Orchard Road:
the season for baseball and lemonade.
But things were much different now.
The faraway war had come as close
as the house next door.
Kids on our street said:
"Remember the time..." or
"Remember when..."

Every story we told about Ted Walker
became a story we never wanted to forget.
Every story seemed important enough to keep.

I'd outgrown my Sunday-best shoes months before.
I put them carefully on a shelf
with my books and my paint box.
Those shiny black shoes
were only a small part of the many important stories.
But they belonged just to me.

Some mornings,
Sam and I saw Ted's mother
working alone in her garden
or taking long walks with Buttons
on Orchard Road.
I told Sam:
"Sometimes it's best to be by yourself
when you're missing someone…"
Sam pulled his cap down low over his eyes
and nodded.

On August 14, 1945,
the war was finally over.
The war was over, over, over!
Now everyone could come home.
Around the world,
soldiers and sailors in all the countries
returned to their families
and their neighborhoods.
Peace.
Another small word
for such a big thing.

Up and down our street
the radios blared with news
and victory music.
I sat on Mrs. Walker's steps with Sam
and tossed a ragged ball to Buttons and said:
"This is the best news in a long time . . .
except Ted won't be coming back . . ."

School began at Beechwood like it always did.
Now I was a fifth grader.
Mrs. Linsay's map of the world
was still there, water blue,
with the continents and the oceans.

I stood in the hallway
and thought about the next-door neighbors
on both sides of the war
who hadn't come home.
So many many neighbors.
I didn't say any words.
I just kept them inside.

I walked up the hall past the big map
and looked for my teacher from last year.
There she was,
ready to greet her new fourth graders,
ready to teach them important things.
When Mrs. Linsay saw me,
she came over and gave me a hug.
We stood together, looking at the blue Pacific.
Then she asked me:
"Ready for fifth grade, Crenshaw?"
"You bet," I said.
And I gave her a thumbs-up.

The war years on Orchard Road
and Mrs. Linsay's map of the blue Pacific
are now far behind me.
Sam and I are all grown up,
with families and streets of our own.
But whenever I see a frisky border collie,
I remember Buttons
and the sketches I drew on two dozen
envelopes.
In every season, especially winter,
I remember Mrs. Walker who lived next door,
and Ted,
the handsome young navy man
who taught me how to shine my Sunday-best
shoes.
And I think about how, all over the world,
the stories are passed down
in different ways and in different voices
from family to family,
and from neighbor to friend . . .
the stories
that are important enough to keep.

AUTHOR'S NOTE

*P*art of this story is based on fact. My uncle Theodore Taylor Walker, whom I never knew, graduated from the United States Naval Academy at Annapolis in February of 1941. While there, Ted Walker captained the 1940 cross-country team, which was undefeated. He served aboard a cruiser, the USS *Memphis,* in the South Atlantic, and later, as the executive officer of the USS *Albacore* (SS-218, Hugh Rimmer, commander). This submarine completed many war patrols, damaging enemy ships and sinking others including *Taiho,* Japan's newest and largest aircraft carrier.

On October 28, 1944, *Albacore* left Midway Island on its eleventh patrol, headed for the dangerous Japanese waters off northeast Honshu, where four of her sister ships had already disappeared. It was to return to Midway around December 12. When the *Albacore* had not been sighted or heard from by December 21, despite the Navy's watchful lookout for her, the submarine was presumed lost.

Several years after the war, the Walker family learned the details of the *Albacore*'s last patrol from official naval records. The submarine hit a mine on November 7, 1944, in the Sea of Japan near Esan Misaki (latitude 41°, 49'N, longitude 141°, 11'E). The Japanese minesweeper *Fukuei Maru No. 7* reported seeing three explosions in the water. A rudder, hydroplane, some books, a tobacco pouch, and floating debris rose to the surface. My uncle was twenty-three years old at the time of his death. The USS *Albacore* and the names of her eighty-six crew members are honored at the Submarine Memorial in Honolulu, Hawaii.

During a school visit in 1993, I happened upon a world map in a hallway at St. Teresa's School in Cincinnati, Ohio. This map had been painted in 1944 by an eighth grade student, Mary Caruso. I included her remarkable map as an element in my story since events that happened in the Pacific Ocean must have seemed a world away from a neighborhood street in America.